The Little Green Witch

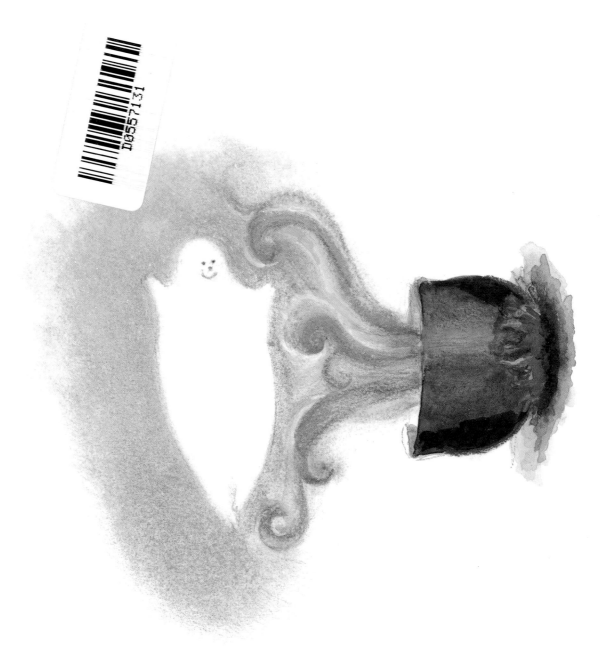

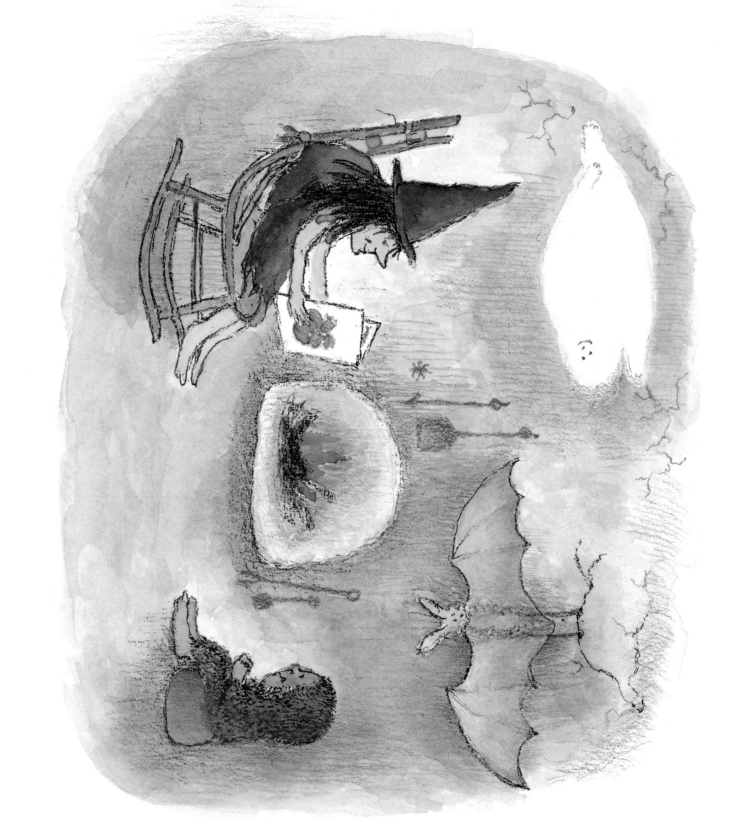

The Little Green Witch

Barbara Barbieri McGrath  Illustrated by Martha Alexander

Charlesbridge

Love to my daughter Emily, my favorite witch, and my son Louis, my favorite gremlin.

Special thanks to Dominic "water schmater" Barth; Emily Mitchell, a wise witch; and Susan Sherman, for her "magic" touch.—B. B. M.

For Jane, Ginnie, and Jan.—M. A.

First paperback edition 2006
Text copyright © 2005 by Barbara Barbieri McGrath
Illustrations copyright © 2005 by Martha Alexander

Published by Charlesbridge
85 Main Street
Watertown, MA 02472
(617) 926-0329
www.charlesbridge.com

Library of Congress Cataloging-in-Publication Data
McGrath, Barbara Barbieri, 1954–
  The little green witch / Barbara Barbieri McGrath ; illustrated by Martha Alexander.
    p. cm.
  Summary: The little green witch's three friends are too lazy to help her tend the pumpkin seeds she has planted, but when they all want to eat the pumpkin pie that she makes, the witch exacts her revenge.
  ISBN-13: 978-1-58089-042-7; ISBN-10: 1-58089-042-3 (reinforced for library use)
  ISBN-13: 978-1-58089-153-0; ISBN-10: 1-58089-153-5 (softcover)
  [1. Folklore.] I. Alexander, Martha G., ill. II. Little red hen. III. Title.
PZ8.1.M176Li 2005
[398.2]—dc22   2004018948

Printed in the United States of America
(hc) 10 9 8 7 6 5 4 3 2
(sc) 10 9 8 7 6 5 4 3 2

Illustrations done in watercolor, color pencil, and pastel
Display type and text type set in Mayflower, designed by P22 and Adobe Caslon
Color separations by Imago
Printed and bound by Lake Book Manufacturing, Inc.
Production supervision by Brian G. Walker
Designed by Susan Mallory Sherman

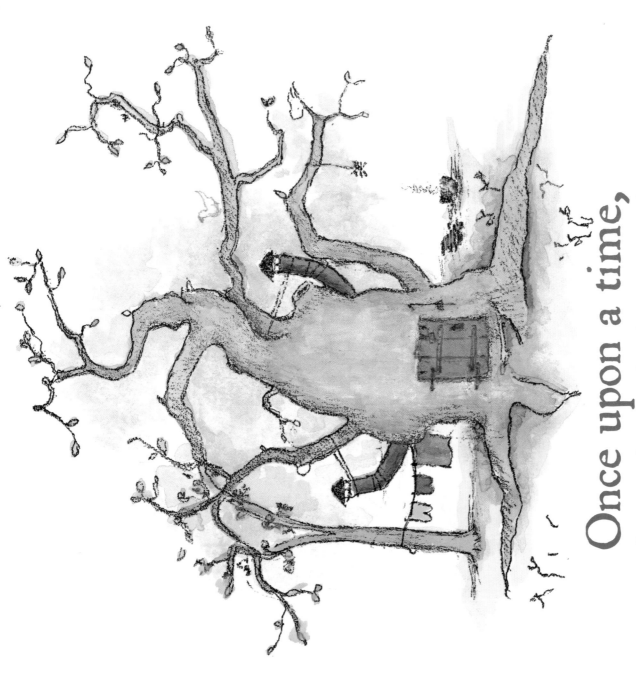

Once upon a time,

deep in the woods, there was a ghost,
a bat, a gremlin, and a little green witch.
They all lived together in a twisted
hollow tree.

The ghost liked to float lazily
above the steaming cauldron.

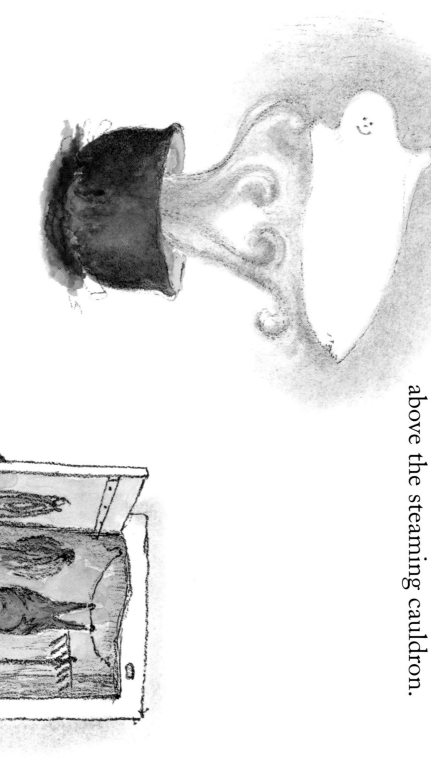

The bat liked to hang around,
snoozing in the broom closet.

The gremlin liked to nap in the dark, damp cupboard under the sink.

So the little green witch did all the unhousework.

She stirred the brew, spread the soot,
and hung the cobwebs.

She mixed the potions and
dirtied the laundry.

She shook the trees, scattered the leaves and twigs,
and pulled the unsightly flowers in the garden.

One day she found some pumpkin seeds amid the muck. "Just what I need!" she said.

"Who will help me plant the pumpkin seeds?"
asked the little green witch.

"Not I," said the ghost.

"Not I," said the bat.

"Not I," said
the gremlin.

"Then I will do it myself," grumbled the little green witch.

"Who will help me water the seeds?" asked the little green witch.

"What, me?" asked the ghost.

"Beg your pardon?" asked the bat.

"Water, schmater," grouched the gremlin.

So each morning she watered the pumpkin seeds. Soon pumpkin vines pushed through the ground and spread across the yard. Pumpkins began to grow big and round.

When the pumpkins were ripe and ready
to pick, the little green witch hissed,
"Who will help me pick the pumpkins?"

"Not now," said the ghost.

"Can't hear you," said the bat.

"That leaves me," growled the little green witch.

"Go away," said
the gremlin.

After picking the pumpkins, the little green witch screeched, "Who will help me scoop the yuck and gloop from the pumpkins?"

"Nope," said the ghost.

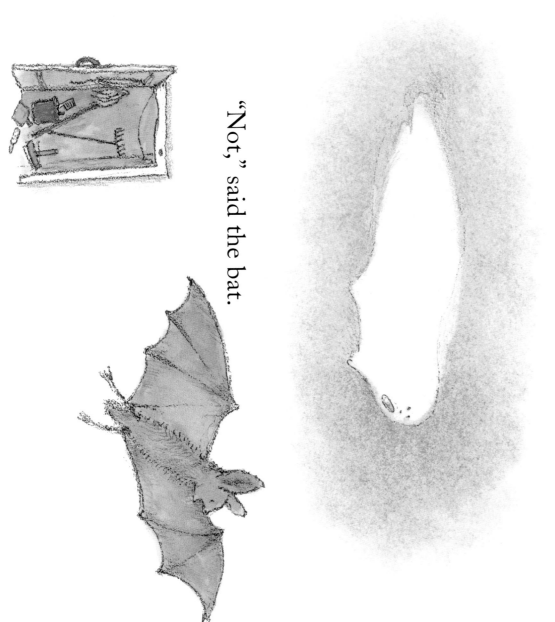

"Not," said the bat.

"Very funny," said the gremlin.

"Why did I bother asking?" groaned the little green witch.
She shook her head, disgusted with the three of them.
Then she scraped out the pumpkin gloop.

"Who will help me carve the pumpkins? As if I didn't know," howled the little green witch.

"No way!" said the ghost.

"Not likely!" said the bat.

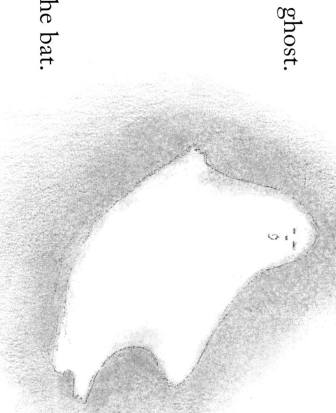

"Oh, do go away!"
said the gremlin.

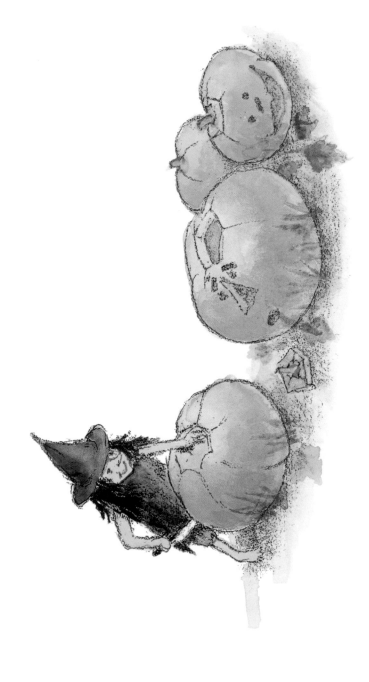

"I'm on my own again," sighed the little green witch.
And she carved the pumpkins.

Then from the gloop she took out the seeds and mashed and squashed and chopped. She added sour flour, monster molasses, and an ostrich egg.

Then the little green witch poured the mush into a piecrust and popped it in the oven.

Soon the twisted tree began to reek of horrible, monstrous pumpkin pie.

The ghost drifted out of the steam.

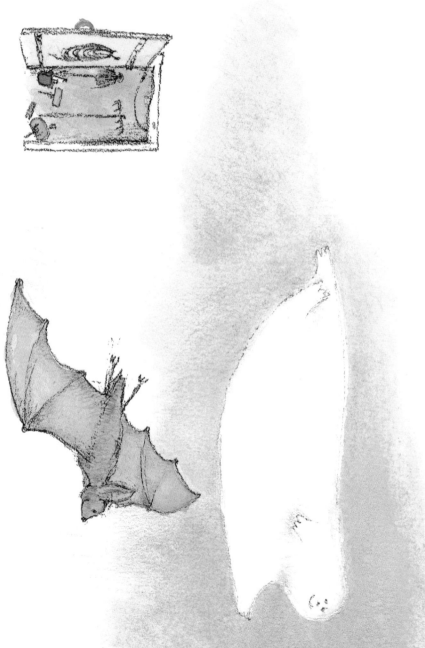

The bat flew out of the broom closet.

The gremlin shook off the dishrags and sloshed out from under the cupboard.

Then, when it was nicely burnt, the little green witch took the pie from the oven.

In her sweetest, scratchiest voice, she asked, "Who wants some pie?"

"I do!" said the bat.

"I do!" said the ghost.

"Don't bother with a fork!" said the gremlin.

But the little green witch smiled her gruesome smile and said, "I planted the seeds. I watered the pumpkins. I carved the pumpkins. I mashed the pulp. I made the pie.

"And now I'm going to eat the pie myself. But before I do—"

The little green witch raised her arms, waved her wand, and—POOF!

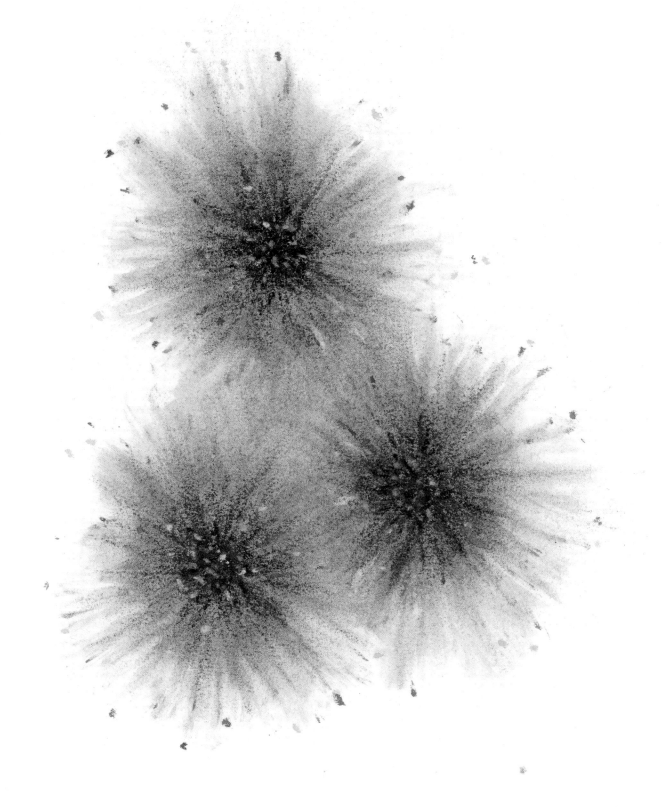

—turned the ghost, the bat, and the gremlin into…

...little red hens.